This item was purchased for the Library
through Zip Books, a statewide project of the
NorthNet Library System and Califa Group,
funded by the California State Library.

Brief, horrible moments

A collection of one sentence horror stories

Written by:
Marko Pandza

Table of contents

Foreword

Horrible moments are often brief. The realization. The utterance. The pain. The shock. The news. The accident. The monster. The thing we fear most made real.

But the aftermath of horrible moments, for me, is the truly scary part. The part we don't yet understand. The part we can't quite fathom.

This collection contains the sum of my own fears, both real and imagined, not only in the words on the page, but in what they suggest. I want you to wonder as I have, *what comes next?*

I sincerely hope for the both of us that whatever moments are yet to come, they aren't too horrible. And yes, that includes reading these stories.

Monsters, demons, creatures and oddities

It laid its hands on my shoulders, still staring at me from across the lake.

Frozen in terror, I watched the head emerge from the cave's mouth, rolling towards the forest to greet its returning body.

I narrowly escaped the beast, its countless claws scratching at the door I'd just barely shut, but I breathed a sigh of relief, turned around and discovered there were more of them.

"You can trust me," whispered the voice of my childhood best friend from deep within the bathtub's drain.

As I looked out over the field to check on the brewing storm, I caught one of the scarecrows falling off its perch, blaming strong winds until it began walking towards me.

I could tell it was looking at me, even though there wasn't a single eye in its heads.

The elongated figure was still clutching the knife, still right behind me, still reminding me that I couldn't outrun my own shadow.

The man continued running his fingers up and down the balloon, producing a sharp squeaking sound that would have been annoying, rather than terrifying, had the balloon not been sitting where his head should have been.

I had written off the stranger at my door as a mere salesman, but I understood he likely wasn't a man at all when he opened his briefcase and removed an itemized list of every secret I ever had.

All my friends knew I slept during the day because I worked the night shift, which was easier than explaining that I'd been given a curfew by the thing in my closet.

The towering abomination lurched towards me, its filthy feet leaving a trail of footsteps on both the floor and the ceiling.

The last strip of my scalp peeled away and dropped to the floor before me, and just as I'd begun thinking the worst of the torture was over, the claw pushed my head down and whispered: "eat."

"Please, don't do this!" the creature repeated, still mimicking my screams, only this time it finally had my voice right and tossed me effortlessly into the grave it had dug.

I lay on my back atop the spongy red cushion, trembling in the darkness at the fact that the roof above my head belonged to a mouth.

The locked window kept the crooked, emaciated thing at bay, but unfortunately for me, its shadow was still free to enter.

The moment her sparkling emerald eyes met mine, I was frozen in place, transfixed by the realization that everything below my waist had already turned to stone.

I felt the warm, sensual touch of a tongue licking its way up my neck, which I might have enjoyed had it been attached to a person.

I entered the room to find it standing in the corner, and I was still trying to figure out where the top half of it had gone when the door closed behind me.

I awoke struggling to catch my breath, unsure of why my sleeping bag was so tight until I tried pulling it down and felt the scaly exterior swallow the next few inches of my torso.

Normally, I'd be thrilled to see my wife, but I now felt nothing but terror as I gazed into her eyes, which moments ago had become something else's.

The enormous grin stretched from ear to ear and wall to wall.

I pressed the gas pedal to the floor, screaming as we veered into oncoming traffic, but my terror did nothing to diminish the delight of my passenger who hadn't been there when I started the car.

Though she was all ears, I was too frightened to speak, for I'd never seen a body built that way.

The worm's head burst up through the dirt, waving wildly to and fro, each movement sending a ripple of wind through my clothes.

Like most humans, I couldn't remember much from the day I was born, except for emerging from the dirt.

For a moment I thought I'd bumped into the stiff, thin legs of a stilt-walker, but whatever it was, no matter how far back I craned my neck I couldn't see its head.

She was the most beautiful, perfect human I'd ever seen, except that she wasn't one.

The smiling clown looked into my eyes, clutched my broken, twisted body and whispered: "I'm going to make you a balloon animal."

It was an ungodly hour to hear a knock at the front door, which I regretted opening as soon as I saw the face, if it could be called that, considering the complete absence of features.

I'd seen some big eaters, but the man staring at me and hungrily licking his lips was the size of a small house.

Group hugs were usually comforting, but not this time, since all six arms belonged to the same person.

Thirst finally quenched, she pried her mouth from my spurting wound, but I knew she wasn't done, only waiting for me to replenish.

The frigid forest was pitch black, only heightening the sensation of the twigs brushing against my cheeks and the sound of the voice rasping: "I'm sick of buttons and carrots, I want a real face."

No matter how fast I ran, I could still hear the heavy, pounding sounds of footsteps right behind me, but however many times I turned around, I still couldn't see what was making them.

The elevator doors closed on my body, which would have been painless had they not just unsheathed their teeth.

There was no doubt that the fall had broken my spine; only seconds ago I was looking into the hole that had materialized in my backyard, so afraid of what might come out of it that I didn't consider something might pull me in.

I had an enviable body, so I was never afraid to be naked in front of a woman, until I met one who removed her dress and took her skin with it.

I hadn't the slightest clue what substance the spewing beast had covered me with, but I was sure that the wet, bubbling pile at my feet was my skin.

Quickly growing confident in my newfound ability, I soared through the air and touched clouds for the first time in my life, utterly fearless until the voice above me said: "I'm going to drop you now."

Innumerable years after being imprisoned in darkness by forces outside my control, I allowed the bright, warm sunlight to envelop my body for a precious few seconds before I burst into flame.

If you didn't count the doll's face and the fact that it was the size of a truck, it was a regular looking spider.

His two big, blue eyes stared deeply into mine, but his thousand yellow ones didn't.

I must have stabbed him at least a hundred times, but he was still laughing.

Pulling the long black hair out from the drain didn't bother me until I realized it was attached to something.

I was crouched in the dark alley, petting the soft fur and listening to that gentle purr, wondering why someone would discard such a beautiful creature when as if on cue, its stinger emerged.

The creature pulled its own head upwards,
separating it from the body with great gouts of
blood, then turned until our eyes met and gurgled:
"I'd prefer yours."

The face of the thing peering through my bedroom
window didn't really scare me until its hands emerged
from under my bed.

Murder, death and the dead

My father was causing a scene as usual, slurring his words and attacking pew after pew of terrified mourners who had gathered for his funeral.

I was in the meat locker, unhooking the next carcass when I ran into my shift supervisor, who should have been on vacation, as well as right side up.

The body on the autopsy table was riddled with bullet wounds, large chunks of flesh missing and his face more mush than man, and yet, he was halfway to standing back up.

I was shivering, soaked head to toe, hearing her say something about starting a nice warm fire, but I was too overwhelmed by the fumes to notice her striking the match.

The skin on both my hands felt tight, like skin often does after a sunburn, so I continued searching my collection for a better fitting pair.

I was anxious to reach my destination on time, sighing with relief when I heard the train approaching before taking my seat between the tracks.

When I saw those dead eyes staring back at me, I let out an involuntary shriek and slammed the door, for that was the last thing I expected to see in my date's fridge.

I stared out over the cliff to the gorgeous view, her gentle hands on my shoulders, but I only realized why she'd insisted the hike would be worth it once she pushed.

The fact that my boyfriend made such a good living off his handmade lampshades was less surprising than how long it took for someone to notice the freckles.

Impossibly tight and well out of earshot, the abandoned home's crawlspace was the most perfect hide and seek spot Stephen had ever found; not a single mourner disagreed.

I'd always known birth was painful, but what I hadn't known was that the mothers kept screaming long after you'd cut it out.

One whiff of the decayed stench coming from the basement and I was drenched in cold sweat, not for fear of what might be causing it, but because it reminded me of what I'd done.

I trembled as I peered through the closet's slats, watching it breathe heavily, until I decided it was time to finish off my victim.

The barber brought out his straight razor, ready to begin shaving the face of the unfortunate woman strapped to his chair.

It's fun blowing bubbles, just not while living out your final moments underwater.

I didn't remember much about before I was taken from my parents, but I knew I was smarter than any of the kids in my new school when I got an A+ for my class project, whose brains were still oozing out onto the floor.

I had never crowd surfed before, and just when I was starting to enjoy the feeling, I was lowered to the ground, allowing everyone the chance to trample me as planned.

My husband was half an hour into a well-deserved soak in the steaming tub, but his skin was only just beginning to prune, so I decided I needed stronger acid.

Among the worst parts of finding myself dangling from the noose was that it wasn't tied to anything.

The butcher hacked at the meat, holding out a fresh cut for me to inspect, asking me if I wanted to select which part of my body was next.

I watched the lifeless face through the flames as I had countless times before, except this time, it was from the wrong side of the cremation oven's door.

I stayed after class because mummy told me to always be nice and Mrs. Chadwick was crying and said I was sweet and she just had a bad day but I didn't want her to cry so I made her stop and now she can never cry again.

I reached out as she fell, managing to get a firm grip on her hand, but it was no use, since my feet had already left the cliff's edge.

"I'm a bit of a celebrity," he repeated, but this time, she believed him, his handsome face appearing on the TV screen right next to those of his victims.

The magician began sawing the woman in half, and I was utterly amazed at how long she stayed alive.

When I entered the den, I found my liquor cabinet ransacked and my estranged father sipping a full glass of scotch, eyeing me from the armchair in the suit I buried him in.

Fate was indeed cruel, for I soon realized the first person I ever killed turned out to be the very last person on Earth.

My boyfriend terrifies me; he's been stalking me ever since I killed him.

There wasn't a better player in the tournament, but it had been rigged against me; I hadn't thrown a single dart before they mounted me on the wall and began.

I hungrily inhaled her scent, which was even more intoxicating than the other times I'd dug her up.

The rotting corpse was like a human pincushion,
a wide assortment of knives jutting out at all
angles, which would have been horrifying even if
it wasn't shambling towards me.

Even before I laid my cards down I could sense I
had been bested, keenly aware that this defeat
would be a bitter pill to swallow, considering the
contents were mostly cyanide.

Henry lived by his conviction until he grew old:
that ending another man's life was unforgivable,
unless you skinned him first.

My step-father's sobbing pleas did nothing to stop my hands from squeezing his windpipe, and though I managed to loosen my grip for a moment, my own pleas didn't either.

I'd seen a skyscraper's rooftop from an airplane window before, just not seconds before seeing a pedestrian up close.

"If we want to survive these woods, we *have* to stay together," I shouted at my panicked friends, relieved when they agreed since it would be much easier than picking them off seperately.

I joyfully dove headfirst into the lake, my
screams unheard by those above water when I
discovered what remained of that missing boy.

He waved to me from the balcony, and I waved
back, watching the fire I set work its way up to
his floor.

Family, friends, love and relationships

38

Nothing could tear us apart; she'd sewn too many parts of us together.

I'd been burned, buried, shot, stabbed, drowned and disemboweled, but no matter how much they tried, my family couldn't save me from what I'd become.

My mom tucked me in, kissed my forehead and told me she loved me, which was when I knew something had taken her place.

"We're going to be a family," I whispered as I observed the smiling faces of my future wife and son from outside the house.

My friends warned me that he was two-faced, but I didn't believe them until the real one ripped itself free.

I felt my husband's warm arms wrap around me from behind, which would have been comforting if I hadn't been laying across from his cold body.

She hugged me tighter, soothingly hushing my cries until with a loud *crack*, she absorbed my broken body into hers.

My wife was silent and obviously furious as we pulled away from the daycare, but I had to check the back seat to confirm the very thing I couldn't convince her of: that the adorable little freckle by our daughter's nose had changed sides.

"I don't usually go this far on a first date," she giggled, briefly letting me gasp for air before pushing my head back underwater.

It was an awkward reunion; after all, we hadn't seen each other since he died.

I stroked her hair and ran my thumb gently across the down of her temples before I kissed her for the first time, deeply, eager for the rest of her body waiting on the other side of the room.

I followed the trail of dirt and footprints until I found my husband setting up a camera in the living room while inviting me to take my place for our annual family portrait to the left of our putrefied son.

She had nervously insisted on turning off the lights first, and as I kissed my way up from her body to her lips, she finally found the courage to touch one of my tentacles.

"I didn't get in," I told my parents after reading the letter in silence, and as supportive as they acted, I knew that even if I did, they still wouldn't have let me leave my cage.

The escalator was moving smoothly, its machinery unimpeded, which was unfortunate since it had already ground half my friend's body to a pulp.

Though my new husband forbade it, I took his
absence as an opportunity to explore his expansive
trophy room, admiring the atrocious beauty and
stroking the heads of countless well-preserved
beasts until my hands came upon an empty mount
with my name on it.

I now knew the tree was a terrible place to hide
from the storm, and if ash could speak, my friends
would have agreed.

"You'll be going home with them," my foster
mother wept, nudging me towards the woman who
pinched my cheeks, looked up to her husband and
hissed: "meatier than the last."

"I want you to look me in the face," my best
friend repeated, but I'd already tried once, and
all that had been there was a ragged, gaping hole.

I was begging her to forgive me, crying, telling her I
didn't want things between us to end like this, but
she'd heard enough, and continued cutting.

My boyfriend's hands tentatively touched my body,
and as he pulled me closer I remembered he'd been
dead for years.

I'd given all the blood I could to save her, my head spinning and my body weak, but I knew it wasn't nearly enough when I saw her lips form one final word: "more."

I watched my wife lift my son off the ground, no different than ten thousand times before, save for setting him gently down on the bear trap.

All my traumatized parents could ever muster was that my brother suffered terribly and had died long before I was born, and the explanation was enough until the day I found him under our house.

I'll never forget the stifling heat as I waved goodbye to my son alongside the rest of the village, watching with a mix of pride and sorrow as he took the final steps of his journey into the volcano.

Standing here at the altar should have been the best moment of my life, but the pale face behind the veil was neither my fiancée nor human.

"I'm so impressed," she shouted when she saw how far I'd squirmed without the use of my arms and legs, and I cried like an infant when she effortlessly carried my limbless torso back to the nursery and whispered: "you've left me little to remove, but I'll make sure you don't leave your crib again."

I had to accept the horror of the fact that though I only looked away from the baby monitor a moment, my bundle of joy had been replaced with a bundle of sticks.

Food and eating

Ignoring the crippling hangover, I desperately counted my fingers hoping they weren't all there, for a missing digit would be a more palatable explanation of what I did last night than the severed one I just threw up.

I had swallowed every bite, but the gnawing, empty sensation of hunger was undiminished, so I turned my eye to the next child.

"The longer you refuse, the longer you'll have to stay here and the more you'll have to eat," it said, dropping a fork next to the massive bowl of dense black hair.

"The Pritchett family is so delighted with you they've asked for seconds," the sous-chef beamed as he re-entered the kitchen, asking as he held the butcher knife to my remaining leg: "above the knee, or below?"

My friends used to tell me I always bit off more than I could chew, until I proved them wrong and swallowed their kidneys whole.

After a lifelong struggle with weight loss, I was thrilled to discover a method that worked for me and quickly prepared to cut away the next pound of flesh.

Still chained to the wall, my skeleton clearly
visible through my starving body's skin, I tried
chewing the stale bread before me again, but the
moment I swallowed, it was back on the plate as if
I'd never touched it.

I did as I was told, crunching the next spoonful of
my breakfast between my teeth, imagining it was
anything but broken glass.

This was the third time finding a hair in my soup,
but only the first time making the connection to
my missing dog.

I had dismissed my wife's recent distance as a passing phase, and the delicious dinner she spontaneously cooked me tonight seemed like proof that it was until I bit into someone's fingernail.

I know this most recent escalation of my eating disorder is killing me, but my insides still feel dirty, and there are more cleaning supplies I have yet to try.

The waiter lifted the silver dome off my plate to reveal another tantalizing dish, glanced from the pristine silverware to my wrist restraints, and prepared to feed me the thirty-first course.

Fear, dread and the unknown

My favourite doll was lying in bed next to me, but I hadn't put her there, nor had I seen her since the night my childhood home burned down.

I woke up in darkness, unable to move, speak or see, remembering the accident only when the coroner unzipped my body bag.

"Its...just the wind," my husband said, explaining away the scraping in the attic again, but this time, the moment's pause was somehow enough to tell me he not only knew *what* was up there, but that he himself had put it there.

"Hello?" I screamed into the night from the centre of the cornfield, and the scary part wasn't that a voice responded, but that an hour ago, over thirty others had.

I was starving and dehydrated, but after what felt like days I finally managed to climb out of the dark hole I had awoken in, straight into the light of a single bare bulb and the bottom of the next hole.

"You have more inside," the knife-wielding mugger hissed, waiting until I finished turning out my empty pockets before narrowing his eyes, raising his knife and clarifying with a smile: "no, *inside.*"

There are some books that just speak to me, but
what they tell me to do terrifies me.

I had long since given up wondering why I was
locked in this tiny box all these years; all I wanted
to know now was why I just couldn't seem to die.

Rigid and motionless before the mirror, I stared as
my own reflection walked towards me.

My sunburn must be well into the third degree,
but even if I had the strength to leave this beach,
the straps are just too tight, and the tide has come
in too far.

One day I simply blinked and that twisted,
shadowy thing appeared, disappeared with the
next blink, returned with the next, over and over,
closer and closer until it whispered in my ear and
vanished with a final flutter of my eyelids; today,
and for the remainder of my days in this white
padded room, I live terrified of the blink that will
bring the thing back to do what it promised.

I hadn't slept in days, and as I lay my head down,
I hoped not to be woken again by the shouting
voice inside my pillow.

I never thanked gravity for keeping my feet firmly on the ground, but I cursed it the day it inexplicably grew enough to allow me to see Hell.

One moment, Teresa was floating in the resort pool, easing into a nap, and the next, she was floating in the middle of the ocean with no shoreline in sight, confident she would soon wake up until she remembered she already had.

"All you have to do is flick this switch whenever you see the red light," he said, backing out of the bunker with the gun still trained on me, but I knew he'd left out the three most important words: *until, you,* and *die.*

I accepted there was nowhere to run, pressing my back against the wall and waiting for the other three to press against me.

I always wanted the best of both worlds, until the night I awoke to find myself trapped in the other one.

The septic tank was full, and I wished I had emptied it when I had the chance, now that I was so close to drowning.

"You can run now," said the inhuman voice after one last deep sniff of my laundry.

I realized as I approached the car that I didn't want my camping trip to end, and as I tried desperately to find my keys, I knew the clown emerging from the woods didn't either.

Everything from my neck down tingled like it was asleep, which I desperately wished was the case as I watched them pour the next bucket of centipedes into the well.

"I'll see you in Hell," the well-dressed stranger said with a knowing smile before vanishing in the same blink that revealed my room had become a charred version of itself.

The cage in front of me was swarming with at least a thousand scorpions, and though it was one of the zoo's most horrifying displays, I would have happily taken that over what was in mine.

The growing shadow moved up the wall adjoining the staircase in lockstep with the loudening creaks of the old wooden stairs, but otherwise, whatever was coming to greet me wasn't something I could see.

I woke up feeling drugged, paralyzed, barely comprehending that my left hand was stretching one of my eyelids open while my right clutched a nail and crawled its way up the ropes they'd both tied.

I stared at the faces in the mirror; last time I'd checked, I only had one.

Clutching the bloody hammer, I walked carefully past the unconscious body, my urge to flee outweighed by my curiosity, and only when I'd descended the final step into the basement did I hear the door slam shut and lock behind me.

"She's a beaut, huh?" he asked, revving the engine with pride, as if I'd dare bruise the ego of a man wielding a chainsaw.

The thing cordially introduced itself, its name so much like that of a place I'd recently heard of, and it dawned on me that what it was and where I was standing were one and the same.

I never considered swimming in neck deep lake water scary until I was forced to try it while staring out my car windows.

Like everyone who followed the news, I was watching the broadcast rumoured to be the Bayside Butcher's next live skinning, but all I could see onscreen was black until I flicked on my desk lamp, illuminating the inside of my closet.

My eyes took a while to adjust to the cluttered basement's darkness, and even when they did, I was sure I had bumped into a mirror until the growl told me the eyes I was looking into didn't belong to me at all.

I dove off the dock with a squeal of delight, eager for the first swim of the season, only noticing on my way down that the lake was boiling.

I had always been afraid of the darkness, but never more so than tonight, when whatever was in it finally spoke.

This morning, my lifelong fear of leaving the house saved me, because whatever was out there now, it wasn't people.

Something was pulling me by the ankle, though I couldn't see what, since my entire leg was already inside the storm drain.

I pulled the ripcord, elated at scratching this one last item off my bucket list, only realizing when I saw the holes how appropriate the timing was.

I trained for the race like my life depended on it, only to find it truly did when they revealed my opponent was a younger me.

The intricately carved music box had both started and stopped playing on its own, and the sudden absence of that sweet melody coaxed me to touch it, a choice I regretted when I saw the blackness travelling visibly upwards through the veins in my hands.

I was slowly enveloped in darkness, not because the blazing sun was setting, but because the black bubble was closing on me.

"Turn around," came the whisper in an all too familiar voice: my own.

Shark diving had been a lifelong dream, and as I was lowered past the chum into the churning waters, I wished there was a cage.

I was sure now the bed used to be on my right, and as I returned my own gaze in the mirror before me, I wondered at which precise moment I had become the reflection.

I'd seen everyone I ever knew torn apart and put on display, all manner of twisted abominations, and swarms of vile, writhing creatures, but the worst part of my nightmare was that I was wide awake.

I can't decide which is worse: the clown outside my bedroom window, or the fact that I live on the fifth floor.

I scrambled to keep my footing on the ledge, desperate to avoid my worst fear, but the pavement was already racing towards me, just as it had after every other time I'd hit the ground.

I was worried when I saw the elderly gentleman trip, but my heart leapt into my throat when his frail body hit the pavement and exploded into a swarm of flies.

I woke up in the dark, feeling my way around the tiny room to a wooden door, beating against it until to my surprise, the wood gave way, enveloping me in dirt and the knowledge that I'd been buried vertically.

I nearly pissed myself when my wife's voice suddenly called my name from behind me while she was still standing right in front of me.

I went down to the basement when I heard my daughter's boisterous giggle, finding her with an ear pressed to a vent and mouthing: "I hear it too."

As I watched the levitating glass of water return to the table, I assumed the spirit was simply announcing its presence, but by the time my body was halfway to the clouds, I knew it had simply been warning me of its power.

Only once I had walked by for the third time did I believe was I was seeing: the eyes in the painting were following me.

I reached down to rub my legs free of the sudden cascade of pins and needles, but when the stabs of pain began, I saw that my problem wasn't poor circulation, just bees.

Crime and punishment

I couldn't understand a word the guards were saying to each other apart from *tourist*, but though I had done nothing wrong, I could tell the conversations had escalated when one of them opened my cell clutching a hammer and nails.

"That's an ugly child," the woman said as she pointed at my little girl before removing the knife from her purse, and as we ran, I pined for a time when being anything less than beautiful wasn't a crime.

I went into shock at about the same time I lost sight of the two police cruisers pulling away with my hands still cuffed to the bumpers.

Every day like clockwork, he visits my cell just to
scratch a new number into the wall, always
leaving with a smirk that reminds me I have no
clue what he's counting down to.

Most of the other guys who defrauded the
company had already gotten the axe, so I was
surprised when they told me I was one of the
lucky few getting the guillotine.

The wicker box was as beautiful inside as it had
appeared on the outside, if you didn't count the
scorpions.

"Good dog," I said, satisfied that the last brutal yank of the choke chain had finally made him sit and stop begging, except for one last pathetic whimper: "*please*, stop."

When I regained consciousness my cheek felt like it was resting upon a hard pillow, then I saw my smiling wife and kids at the head of the roaring mob and remembered I had been sentenced to the chopping block.

The closer I got to the podium, the more my hands shook; public speaking was scary enough without having to sway a mob of paying strangers to spare your life.

Doctors, health and hospitals

The dermatologist's only explanation for the bubbly, blistered patch on my skin was an allergic reaction, but we both knew it was a weak one when the skin broke and the antennae emerged.

"The surgery was routine," the doctor told me, adjusting the IV as I awoke to the sight of my own face.

"I'm afraid the migraines were a warning sign," he said, holding out the x-rays for me to see seconds before it burst from my skull.

"Don't worry," I reassured her once she noticed the fresh Caesarean scar, "I replaced it with something better."

Throughout my steady decline she had tended to me with patient love and care, but tonight something compelled me to split open one of my pills and pour the contents into my palm, which only seconds later began smoking.

Just after I sneezed, I could feel my stinging eyes turning bright red, just as the rest of the waiting room's had before the blood began to pour.

I knew the treatments would make me feel better eventually, but as I looked at the puddle of blood I had coughed up, I still wished I didn't see so many larvae.

After much debate, the hospital's chief surgeon decided the best course of action was for my arms and legs to be amputated; whatever was next, they didn't want me fighting back.

"The water," Jeff muttered, then moaned, then screamed as the parasite ripped its way out of his gut, and only then did it occur to me we had both drunk from the same well.

"I haven't felt this confident in years," I said to Dr. Hill, admiring my new teeth in the mirror, relieved that inserting them had been easier than taking them from him.

I finally found the strength to leave my blood stained mattress to check the news, only to find the same horrid sickness had already spread to half the continent and the hunt was on for Patient Zero: me.

The human body

My body was all muscle, burning intensely with the effort of what I'd just put it through, but it was worth it to see the full length of my skin without a mirror.

I gasped when my cell mate sliced open his arm, screamed when the insects emerged from the wound, and fainted when they obeyed his order to crawl back in.

I took the man's outstretched palm, fearing nothing of a simple handshake until I couldn't let go, not because I didn't want to but because our hands had already fused together.

The bubbling water's heat was pleasant, almost like a hot tub, until my skin began to blister and high above me, the lid of the pot closed.

I never believed in the Tooth Fairy, but had let my mother place my first baby tooth under the pillow anyway, sleeping soundly until I woke to the taste of her rusty pliers as she whispered: "not enough."

My head hurt so bad I didn't think I could go on, but everyone in the audience had paid good money to see me perform, so I forced myself to push the drill the rest of the way in.

"We need something to throw on the fire," Grant insisted, chopping with all his might, despite how little of my shivering body remained.

I was close to suffocating, so I jammed my fingers down my throat to scoop out the blockage, only to feel another set of fingers pushing back.

"Babe, your nails grow back so fast," she said, but though I tried again to refuse the manicure, she was already clamping the pliers and preparing to yank.

I'd seen my legs every day of my life, but this was the first time I'd seen them from ten feet away.

I decided my wife had been right in calling me paranoid for taping the garbage disposal's switch, and only when I was forearm deep in the drain in search of her lost wedding ring did I hear the *click*.

My ankles bled, leaving a trail that stretched back as far as the eye could see, too far to tell how long I'd been walking, let alone at which point my feet had ground away.

I scratched harder, but even when I reached muscle, I found no relief from the burning itch, just the eggs.

I was so tired of the rat race; no matter which one finished first, they all got a chance to gnaw at my remaining flesh.

"Smile," she whispered to me in that sweet hypnotic voice, and when she saw how easily I obeyed, she added *wider* and watched as my cheeks split.

My hands shook at first, but I soon got the hang of sewing, and by the time I snipped the sutures that securely sealed my lips, I was confident the process would go just as smoothly with the rest of my body's openings.

"I can't be blind," I sobbed, unable to believe that I'd lost my eyes simply because someone else had wanted them.

I stared at my bulging, pregnant belly in disbelief, unprepared to accept that my water had already broken, let alone that the demon had only just left my bed.

Many people aged seemingly overnight, but I was one of the few lucky enough to look in the mirror and see their flesh draw years closer to decay with each and every blink.

"The more life-like the puppet the better," he said as I nodded eagerly in agreement, which I would have done even if he hadn't been tugging the wires.

It was mesmerizing to watch the master craftsman work, tanning the hide with a kind of grace that almost made me forget I'd been the unwilling donor.

"We barely contained the...rat we tested it on, so what do you think it will do to a *person*?" I screamed, slamming my fists on the boardroom table, making the small vial jump, but I knew it would soon hit the market when someone injected my neck from behind and whispered: "we're about to find out."

I puked my guts out onto the floor, certain the night of hard drinking wasn't to blame when my bones followed.

"What a beautiful ending to a camping trip," Jim muttered, staring up at the stars by the roaring fire, but as much as he tried to appreciate those final moments, he couldn't ignore the bear's gnashing jaws any longer.

I had hoped a good hot shower would make me feel better, but wherever the soap washed away, I now saw bone.

My posture had improved, which was a small blessing as well as a completely irrational thought to have as the stake slid up through my body.

Though painless, it was horrible to behold the exposed fat and muscle of my body, and I suddenly understood the reason so-called alien abductions were so rarely reported was that whatever remained walking the Earth was indistinguishable from the real thing.

Every single person in the cafeteria was staring
right at me, and while I normally would have died
of embarassment, I was too busy holding in my
own guts to care.

"Chug, chug, chug," they chanted as they poured
more down my throat, the liquid pooling on the
floor as it spilled from the hole it had already
burned.

"See? Nothing to be afraid of" he said, removing
the needle and plunging it into my other eye.

It would have been horrifying enough waking up surrounded by blood without the fact that it was sitting in glass jars, each one labeled with my name.

Waking up in bed naked with no recollection of the night's debauchery was a normal experience in my life, but it was another experience entirely to do so locked out of my car, in the middle of nowhere, in the dead of winter.

Several scientists wired me into the machine, explaining that the experiment in pleasure would take all of my bodily sensations and multiply them exponentially and infinitely in my mind, but I realized they meant their pleasure when they pricked me with a pin and locked the door.

Though I was halfway through my second box of tissues, they came back dirtier each time I blew my nose, at first with blood, and now, with brain.

I squeezed the blemish from my face, watching the white, gelatinous substance spray across the mirror with my one remaining eye.

He'd warned me that becoming a member of his club would cost an arm and a leg, but I hadn't expected they'd take all four.

The curse had proven itself real, and despite the fact that my remaining bare patch of skin just sprouted thick, matted hair, I knew it wasn't done when my tongue started to itch.

I couldn't understand why my legs were so numb, until I realized the two blurry things an inch from my eyes were feet.

My captor had never so much as touched me until yesterday when he began drawing on my face, and I only wish I had known he was marking where the straps would go on his Halloween mask.

I'd been desperate for the job, so when they hired me I was prepared to give them my blood, sweat and tears, but what I hadn't been prepared to give were my skin, lung, kidney and eyes.

"You'll never see my face again," I screamed at her; she screamed too when I pushed my face into the glowing coals.

At first, I thought it was a sudden, severe case of food poisoning, but I knew I was in serious trouble when I checked the red-streaked toilet to find I'd quite literally shit out my guts.

The knife slipped as I was dicing tomatoes, leaving my knees weak and mind racing as to whether I needed stitches or an exterminator, blood and baby roaches spilling from the wound.

My leg broke, bloodied bone jutting out for me to see, then my leg broke, bloodied bone jutting out for me to see, then my leg broke, and I wondered what I did to deserve being stuck in this time loop.

Also available by Marko Pandza:

Limbo.

This is the story of a man who accidentally becomes Grim the Reaper, the most highly revered killer in Limbo. A place beyond time and space as we know it where psychopaths compete for perverse honour and status as they carry out their deathly duties.

As Grim struggles to hold onto the memories of the life he's lost, he discovers that the insane being who shaped him (and the course of existence itself) may have sinister plans for the one thing he values most.

In Limbo, the end is only the beginning.

Available on Amazon in softcover, hardcover and Kindle editions.

CPSIA information can be obtained
at www.ICGtesting.com
Printed in the USA
BVOW06s0839221017
498337BV00017B/313/P